For John and Joan
J.B.

For my little Arvo, at three months,
three weeks and one day old
A.L.

A special thanks to design whizz Jamie Hammond

First published 2021 by Walker Books Ltd
87 Vauxhall Walk, London SE11 5HJ

2 4 6 8 10 9 7 5 3 1

This book has been typeset in Arapey

Printed and bound in China

British Library Cataloguing in Publication Data: a catalogue record for this book is available from the British Library

ISBN 978-1-4063-8847-3

www.walker.co.uk

WALKER
BOOKS

FSC
www.fsc.org

MIX

Paper from
responsible sources

FSC® C008047

AGENTS OF THE WILD

OF THE WILD

OPERATION SANDWHISKERS

JENNIFER BELL & ALICE LICKENS

PROLOGUE

Walking through the park, Agnes Gamble slipped her trusty "Field Notes" journal out of her pocket, making sure to keep it hidden from her uncle Douglas. If he ever read it, she would have some serious explaining to do. The journal contained her observations about the natural world, as well as reports of her top-secret missions for **SPEARS** – the Society for the Protection of Endangered and Awesomely Rare Species.

Working for an undercover organization was tricky when you were eight years old. Agnes still had to attend school, do her homework and keep her uncle happy by helping with the chores around their flat. What Douglas *didn't* know, was that Agnes spent the rest of her time fighting to protect the planet's wildlife as a highly skilled **SPEARS** agent.

Now, I know what you're thinking:

*"An eight-year-old secret agent?
That's preposterous!"*

But it's true. In
fact, evidence of
Agnes's adventures
could be found all
over the pages of her
journal. There were
crumbs of dried mud
remaining from the
time she'd crash-
landed in the Atlantic

Forest in search of a lost bee; there were
water stains picked up during an Antarctic
blizzard while trying to save a colony of
brainwashed penguins; *and* there were squid-
ink splatters, panda-drool marks, feathers

from a turkey and hairs from a hare, all
left over from her training.

On the back cover there was even a sticky
fried-banana paw print belonging to
Agnes's partner, Agent Attenborough –
the bravest and most sensible elephant
shrew she'd ever met. (Truthfully, Attie
was the *only* elephant shrew Agnes
had ever met, but she was fairly confident
he was the bravest and most sensible of all.)

"Hurry up, Agnes," Douglas called, ahead.
"I can see the exit."

Agnes gazed across the park. In the
sunshine, the grass was a dazzling green.
"Can't we stay a little longer? It's perfect
weather for birdwatching. I've already spotted
two hawfinches and I heard a nightingale a
moment ago."

Douglas snorted. "A nightingale? That's all I need! Birdsong gives me a headache – you know that."

With a sigh, Agnes returned her journal to her pocket and trudged on. It was hard to believe she was even distantly related to Douglas, especially since her late parents, the famous botanists Ranulph and Azalea Gamble, had been secret **SPEARS** agents too.

Agnes wondered whether they'd also kept "Field Notes" journals. She imagined her father's would have been as neat and carefully labelled as the drawers of his rare-seed collection; her mother's would probably have been filled with colourful botanical drawings similar to the tapioca-leaf wallpaper she'd designed for Agnes's bedroom.

Agnes treasured her memories of them and wished she knew more about their time as **SPEARS** agents. If she could only learn what missions they'd been sent on or who their animal partners had been, it might make them feel closer.

CHAPTER ONE

With a watering-can gripped tightly in one hand, Agnes opened her bedroom window and braced herself against the wind. Living twenty-six floors up meant that tending to the plants in her window box was often a blustery affair. She inspected the buds on her scarlet geraniums, which all seemed healthy, and then poked a finger into the soil to check

how moist it was. Over-watering could be as harmful as under-watering, her parents had taught her.

In the distance, she spotted a bird flying strangely. It seemed to be circling the other skyscrapers in the city and peering through their windows like it was searching for something inside. The bird was bigger than a heron, but too far away to see clearly. Curious, Agnes put her watering-can down and ran to the hidden compartment at the back of her wardrobe, where she stored any equipment she had on loan from **SPEARS**. She fetched a small wooden case with brass hinges and opened it up. Inside was a long cylindrical instrument accompanied by a set of lenses. Some of them were black and shiny; others had a strange yellow glow around the rims.

The device was called an aviascope and, like all **SPEARS** technology, it was inspired by the science of nature – in this case, the extraordinary eyesight of birds.

Each lens allowed Agnes to view the world in a different way. She equipped the aviascope with the "eagle" lens and lifted it to her eye.

Eagles could see four to five times as far as humans, so Agnes could use the device to inspect something like a starling's nest on a roof ten streets away. She shifted the aviascope slowly across the skyline and caught sight of the mystery bird whizzing past another tower block. It had a long neck, pinkish-white feathers and a curved black bill.

Agnes frowned. Based on the bird's size and colouring, there was only one species it could possibly be: a lesser flamingo.

But that didn't make sense. Lesser flamingos lived in Africa and India, so what was the bird doing *here*?

Before she could investigate further, she felt her trouser pocket vibrating and remembered she'd stuffed her chromaphone in there. Another piece of **SPEARS** technology, it looked like a small pebble with an undulating rainbow-coloured surface, like the skin of a Caribbean reef squid – its animal inspiration. Using a chromaphone was the securest way for **SPEARS** agents to communicate long-distance. Agnes returned the aviascope to its case and flicked a switch on the chromaphone. The surface colours transformed into a live video image.

A small beady-eyed mammal with an extraordinarily long nose was squeaking at

Agnes. Its velvety fur went from flame-orange on its head to midnight-black on the rest of its body, with small white circles around the eyes.

"Attie?" Agnes tapped on the **SPEARS** communication pin hidden under the neck of her T-shirt, in order to understand what her partner was saying. "Are you OK? I thought you were visiting relatives in Cairo."

Attie shuffled closer to the screen. He was wearing a surprisingly vibrant Hawaiian shirt patterned with bananas. "I am. They're a family of Flower's shrews, a different species to me." In the background, several small brown shrews with shorter noses than Attie were scurrying back and forth inside an earthy burrow. "I just wanted to call to check how you're doing. Have you logged our daily butterfly count yet?"

"First thing this morning," Agnes replied. "I saw two painted ladies, four common blues and a beautiful red admiral."

"Excellent," Attie remarked. "What about our other **SPEARS** duties? Have you practised Agent Shadowbelly's new technique for subterranean stealth? We're meant to have it mastered by the end of next month."

"Yes, several times already." Agnes

offered her partner a reassuring smile. He was an extremely responsible shrew (it was one of the qualities she most admired about him) but it also meant that he found it difficult to relax. "I promise you, Attie, there's nothing to worry about. Everything here is absolutely—"

But before she could finish her sentence, a whirlwind of pale-pink feathers and spindly fuchsia legs came crashing into her geraniums, showering her with scarlet petals.

The lesser flamingo?! Agnes spat a petal out of her mouth and fumbled with her chromaphone.

"Attie, I've got to go! I'll call you later." As she switched off the device, the flamingo gave a shrill squawk.

"Help!" it screeched, frantically flapping its wings. "I'm stuck!"

Agnes spied the problem immediately: one of the flamingo's webbed feet had got wedged in the gap behind the window box. Thinking quickly, she ran to the other side of her bedroom and snapped off a tall, pointy leaf from her aloe vera plant. "If I rub this on your foot, it should slide out," she explained, returning with the leaf, which was oozing a translucent yellow gel. As she applied the goo to the accessible parts of the flamingo's foot, she noticed a small scroll fastened around the bird's ankle.

"It's not working!" the flamingo shrieked.

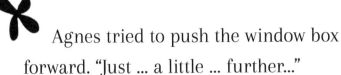

Agnes tried to push the window box forward. "Just ... a little ... further..."

Suddenly, there was a resounding *POP!* and the flamingo's foot shot free. The bird immediately lost its balance, tumbled in through Agnes's bedroom window and landed in a feathery heap in the middle of her carpet.

"Thank you, thank you!" it squawked, scrambling upright.

"Slow down," Agnes urged, as the flamingo hobbled towards the window. "You look injured."

The flamingo shook its head. "Can't stop now. Must deliver urgent message."

The scroll. Agnes wondered how long the flamingo had been flying for. There were deep wrinkles around its orange-red eyes – a sign of dehydration. "If the message is

so important, perhaps I could deliver it for you?" she offered. "That way you can rest and have some water."

The flamingo's feathers ruffled. "You … understand me?"

Agnes was about to explain that she worked for **SPEARS** and was using one of their communication pins when the flamingo gabbled on, "Then you must help me find the Fluffy-Face Cat Food Tower! I've been looking for it everywhere. I'm meant to deliver my message to a turkey named Phil."

"Phil?" Agnes tensed. The Fluffy-Face Cat Food Tower was actually the secret headquarters of **SPEARS** and Phil was no ordinary turkey – he was the fearless Commander of **SPEARS**!

Whatever the flamingo's message was, it had to be important. Agnes held out her hand. "You can give it to me. I know where to go."

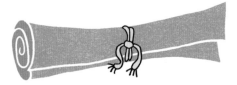

CHAPTER TWO

The lobby of **SPEARS** HQ was noisier than an out-of-tune orchestra warming up for a concert. Agnes raced across the floor with the flamingo's papyrus scroll clutched tightly in one hand, dodging all manner of human and animal agents. Some were hissing,

tweeting or howling into their chromaphones;
others bustled around with toppling stacks of
top-secret case files balanced in their tentacles.
She scanned the crowd and picked out a
friendly-looking chimpanzee wearing a large
rucksack. "Ralph!" she called. "I need cover!"

The chimp turned towards her and raised his hairy eyebrows. With practised speed, he produced a curly wig and a set of human clothes from his rucksack and started dressing himself as he bounded towards the exit.

"Thanks!" Agnes hollered. Ralph was her official chimp replacement – a handy impersonator for whenever she needed to be away on **SPEARS** business. Uncle Douglas hadn't once noticed the difference yet.

With renewed urgency, Agnes hurried towards Commander Phil's office. He was so high-ranking that you normally needed an appointment to see him, but she figured this couldn't wait. She bypassed Bluebell, the Commander's polite but intimidating grizzly-bear receptionist, and knocked on the Commander's big red door. "It's Agent Gamble," she said hurriedly. "I've got an urgent message for you."

A gruff voice said, "Then you'd better come in."

The Commander's office was stuffy with the scents of furniture polish and luxury birdseed. The walls were lined with floor-to-ceiling mahogany bookcases bursting with titles like *The Jungle Book* and *White Fang*. Agnes found the Commander leaning

over his desk, examining a map of Africa. A canvas utility belt was strapped around his black-feathered body.

"Agent Gamble?" The Commander's wrinkly red snood wobbled as he looked up. "What's the message?"

Agnes handed over the scroll and watched with interest as the Commander unravelled it.

"Hmmm." A deep line formed in his wizened brow. "This message arrived with you today?"

"Just now." She briefly explained her encounter with the exhausted flamingo.

"This is bad news, I'm afraid," the Commander told her. "Can you ask Bluebell to set up an emergency meeting in the briefing room? I need to speak with all of our top agents. You included."

Minutes later, Agnes found herself sitting in the second row of the **SPEARS** briefing room, surrounded by several other human and animal agents. It felt odd being there without Attie, but she'd resolved to call him immediately afterwards and explain everything. He would be worrying.

Commander Phil waddled to the front of the room, where a large map of Africa was projected onto the wall. A dozen crosses had been marked across the continent. With an outstretched wing, he pointed to one located in the Eastern Desert of Egypt, between the River Nile and the Red Sea.

"I've just received word that three rock hyrax pups have been abducted from a burrow in Egypt."

Everyone gasped. Agnes recalled what she knew about rock hyraxes. They were very small, stoutly-built mammals with grey-brown fur, rounded ears and long black whiskers. They lived mostly in Africa and the Middle East and spent their time foraging for plants.

"Unfortunately, this isn't the first incident we've heard about," the Commander continued. "In similar cases, leopard cubs have gone missing in Tanzania, rhino calves have been stolen in South Africa and an infant elephant vanished from Botswana. Adults are disappearing too."

Agnes racked her brains, trying to draw a connection between the species mentioned.

Her heart froze when she realized what it might be. "Oh no!" she burst out. "Most of those animals are sought after in the illegal animal trade! Leopards are sold for their fur, elephants for their ivory tusks and rhinos for their horns."

"Exactly." The Commander ruffled his black chest feathers angrily. "As you all know, the illegal animal trade is big business. Animals are poached in order to be sold as exotic pets, or worse, *killed* for their skin and bones."

A chill traced Agnes's spine. Of all the problems **SPEARS** fought against, the illegal trading of animals was one of the most distressing. She imagined how the victims must be feeling, having been snatched from their homes and families.

The terrified infant animals would be missing their parents – a feeling she knew only too well. She tightened her hands into fists, determined to rescue them.

"This spike in cases is extremely alarming," the Commander went on.

"From the details we've gathered, we suspect a single individual is behind it. It could even be someone in the **SPEARS** *Handbook of Known Enemies.*"

The other agents started whispering. The handbook was an essential part of an agent's kit – a "who's who" of environmental villains. With a shiver, Agnes recalled the  last time she'd flicked through its pages. It contained some of the most cunning, cruel and dangerous people on the planet.

An orangutan agent in the back row raised her shaggy arm. "If the animals have all been seized by one person, it's likely they're being held in the same location," she said. "We should follow the clues at the scene of each crime to see where they lead."

The Commander nodded. "I want each pair of agents to investigate one abduction. Working together, we should be able to identify this criminal, shut down their operation and bring them to justice. Most importantly, we need to find those missing animals before it's too late."

Studying the map of Africa, Agnes noticed that the hyrax pups had gone missing not too far from Cairo, where Attie was visiting his relatives. "Commander?" she said, rising to her feet. "I'd like to volunteer to travel to Egypt. If I rendezvous with Agent Attenborough in Cairo, we can travel to the Eastern Desert to investigate the hyrax pups' disappearance."

"Very well," the Commander agreed. Behind him, a long reel of paper started printing out of a strange typewriter surrounded by pink smoke. Once it had finished, he tore it off and handed it to Agnes, who read it through carefully.

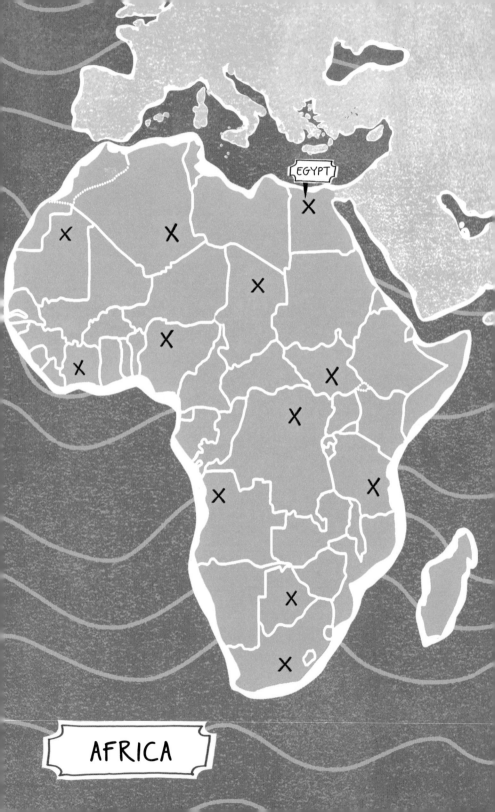

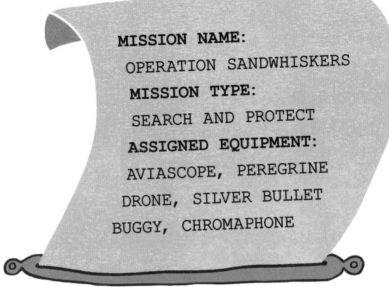

MISSION NAME:
OPERATION SANDWHISKERS
MISSION TYPE:
SEARCH AND PROTECT
ASSIGNED EQUIPMENT:
AVIASCOPE, PEREGRINE
DRONE, SILVER BULLET
BUGGY, CHROMAPHONE

"Good luck, Agent Gamble," the Commander said in a solemn voice. "This may be your most perilous mission yet."

CHAPTER THREE

Agnes's stomach leapt as the peregrine drone
made a sudden dive through the clouds.
"Woooaah!" She clung onto her seat belt as
everything inside the passenger cabin rattled.

The drone was as speedy and as
aerodynamic as its namesake, the peregrine
falcon – the fastest member of the animal
kingdom. Outside, the propellers were

rotating so rapidly Agnes could barely see
them. As blue sky flashed past her window,
she had to remind herself to breathe. She
wondered if this was what it felt like to be
a falcon, soaring and wheeling through
the atmosphere.

Her bottom vibrated as the drone started
to slow. After reaching Cairo, she had piloted
south, following the path of the Nile. Now, far
below, the great river looked like a blue silk
ribbon woven through the lush, green land.

Using her aviascope, she spied softshell turtles resting on the riverbanks, crocodiles lurking in the shallows and purple water hyacinths floating on the surface. The waters, she knew, were home to hundreds of different species of fish, and the river was an important stop-off on a major bird migratory route, which meant that countless species of birds could be seen paddling there throughout the year – lesser flamingos included.

With a pang of sadness, Agnes recalled her parents returning from a trip to Egypt to study papyrus reeds. She considered where they might have camped along the Nile and whether they might've had any encounters with the local wildlife. It was only now she wished she'd asked them more about their experiences; she could have learned so much from them.

As the drone veered east, away from the river, the land turned stony and dry. Agnes watched the drone's shadow pass over the cracked red earth, looking out for signs of spotted hyenas or Nubian ibexes. The Eastern Desert was part of the Sahara, the biggest hot desert in the world, and she'd always been fascinated by the animals that had evolved to cope with the heat and lack of water here.

With a tingle of excitement, she wondered if she'd get the chance to meet some of these ingenious creatures.

Just then, a light flashed on the drone's dashboard. She was ready to land.

"Agent Gamble!" Attie cried from the ground below, waving two landing paddles above his head. A dozen Flower's shrews of all ages were jumping up and down eagerly behind him. "Over here!" He was dressed

in the same pumpkin-coloured uniform as Agnes – a breathable short-sleeved jumpsuit emblazoned with the **SPEARS** logo. Seeing her partner, Agnes felt a surge of confidence. Whatever challenges might lie ahead, she felt sure that the two of them could rescue the stolen hyrax pups and bring to justice the criminal responsible for their abduction.

She set the drone down in a patch of dirt beside a rocky outcrop. As she clambered out, the heat hit her like a blast of flame. Temperatures in this part of Africa could reach fifty-five degrees Celsius, so she grabbed her water bottle. It was important to keep herself hydrated.

With a scratchy patter of feet, the Flower's shrews came scurrying around her

ankles. "Attie's told us all about you, dear,"
squeaked one of the adults.

A trio of youngsters gazed up at Agnes
with large black eyes. "You're bigger than
we thought!"

"Yes, and much less furry," one admitted
with a giggle.

Agnes had to concentrate hard not to tread on any of their tails. "It's nice to meet you all."

"Move aside, move aside!" Attie called sternly, running into the middle of the group. "Agent Gamble and I are on an important mission. We don't have time for chit-chat." He offered Agnes a smile before hurrying over to the peregrine drone to unload their equipment. "First things first: we've got to assemble the silver bullet buggy."

"*Assemble* it?" Agnes repeated. "What on earth do you mean?"

She helped him pull a large case out of the storage compartment. "The peregrine drone can't carry a lot of weight," Attie explained, "so the silver bullet buggy is a light, *flat-pack* desert vehicle, designed to traverse the land at speed."

A flat-pack vehicle? Agnes shook off her surprise, telling herself that she should be used to unusual **SPEARS** engineering by now, and got to work assisting Attie. In no time at all, they'd slotted together a canopied two-seater buggy and were making final adjustments to the large, bouncy wheels.

"Silver bullet..." she murmured, tightening a screw at the rear. She wondered if the buggy took its name from the Saharan silver ant, the fastest ant in the world. They were able to run over one hundred times their own body length in just one second. Even after the exhilaration of the peregrine drone, the idea of moving that fast gave Agnes goosebumps.

As she helped Attie tidy away the last of their tools, she glimpsed a small, dark figure darting through the shadows of the rocky outcrop. It was too big to be a shrew but too fast to be human. Suspicious, she put her screwdriver down and went over to investigate.

"Is everything
all right?" Attie
asked, appearing
at her side.

Agnes furrowed her brow. "I'm not sure. I thought I saw something a moment ago, but ... there's nothing here now."

"Hmmm." Attie inspected the ground. "I can't see any tracks. Perhaps it was a *mirage*?"

Agnes had read about mirages, which were sometimes experienced in deserts. They were optical illusions created when light was refracted in heat haze. "You're probably right," she admitted, feeling her cheeks flush.

"The extreme conditions out here will test us," Attie said sagely. "We just need to stay focused."

Agnes pushed the memory of the shadowy figure to the back of her mind and climbed into the passenger seat of the silver bullet buggy. She wiped the sweat off her brow before fastening her safety helmet and lowering her speed goggles. "The hyrax pups were last seen playing outside their burrow at these coordinates," she said, inputting them into the buggy's navigation system. "Let's go."

With Attie in the driving seat, they waved goodbye to the Flower's shrews and blasted into the desert, leaving a cloud of dust in their wake.

Agnes felt like she was staring into the barrel of a hairdryer as hot air whipped through her hair and into her face. The silver bullet buggy was swift but not very comfortable and she could feel every bump in the ground.

"The report said there were no witnesses around when the hyrax pups were taken," she shouted, the wind snatching her words as she spoke them. "We'll need to scour the area for evidence that someone was there. Anything could be a clue."

By the time they reached their
destination, both agents were covered in a
thick layer of red dust. Attie shook himself
clean as Agnes tried to brush off the worst
of the filth.

"Over there," he said, pointing with his tail to the stump of an old palm tree. Nestled in its roots were three small holes that marked the entrance to the hyrax burrow. There was nothing else around.

"Interesting..." He pressed his long nose to the ground. "I can smell traces of petrol and exhaust fumes – a human car was here."

Elephant shrews had an excellent sense of smell; Agnes didn't doubt that Attie was correct. "I can't see any tyre marks; maybe they blew away."

Attie scratched his chin. "Let's search the area and take notes. We must be able to find something."

Agnes didn't need to be told twice. She pulled out her "Field Notes" journal from her pocket and began scribbling.

OPERATION: SANDWHISKERS
by Agnes Gamble (**SPEARS** Field Agent)

UPDATE:
Scouring the area where the hyrax pups were last seen, Agent Attenborough and I have discovered three possible clues. We are hopeful that at least one of them will lead us to the whereabouts of the missing hyrax pups. Their parents, who are being kept safe in Cairo, must be so worried.

CLUE 1:
ITEM: A scrap of rough brown material.
NOTES: Possibly hessian - a dense woven fabric made from the jute plant. Looks frayed and torn at the edges. Hessian is often used to make ropes and sacks. Perhaps the hyrax pups have been tied up?

CLUE 2:

ITEM: A Peanut Paradiso chocolate bar wrapper

NOTES: Found caught under a rock at the entrance to the hyrax burrow. The inside is coated in residual melted chocolate. Perhaps it was used to lure the hyrax pups away? Or could it be a clue to the kidnapper's diet?

CLUE 3:

ITEM: A business card advertising DIAMOND McGLINTY'S GARAGE

NOTES: The card is dog-eared, suggesting it has been kept in someone's wallet or pocket. The garage address is on the desert road running from the city of Hurghada to the port of Safaga. Could it have been mistakenly dropped by whoever snatched the hyrax pups? We need to visit the garage to find out more.

CHAPTER FOUR

"It's no use," Attie said, shaking the long metal rod attached to the rear of the silver bullet buggy. "The heat has fried our antenna. We'll have to navigate the rest of the way to Diamond McGlinty's Garage ourselves."

Agnes unfurled a map and studied it carefully. It was difficult to pinpoint exactly where they were because the surrounding land had so few markers. "According to this, we need to head south until we meet a wadi – a dry riverbed." After checking her compass, she fetched the aviascope from her pack and loaded the "American woodcock" lens to scan the horizon. American woodcocks had a 360-degree field of vision, so Agnes could now see all around her. To the east lay a long spine of mountains; to the west, a strange khaki-green shape flickered in the haze.

As Attie clambered back into the driving seat, Agnes refitted the "eagle" lens and took a closer look. The khaki-green shape was in fact a large canvas tent, erected over an area of sand. A table outside was covered

with small brushes, hand shovels and spades;
and a young spectacled man dressed in a
loose linen shirt and shorts was relaxing in a
deckchair beside it.

"What can you see?" Attie asked.

"I think it's an archaeological dig site," Agnes guessed. She didn't know much about archaeologists other than what she'd seen on TV, but she was sure they used tools to excavate historical sites, and Egypt had lots of those.

Attie fastened his seat belt and started up the engine. "In that case, I suggest we ask for directions."

As they drove closer, the young man in the deckchair jumped up and started waving. "Oh, please do be careful where you're driving!" he called. He had a freckled face and scruffy blond hair. "The land here is very fragile. There are ancient tombs hidden below the surface!"

"Thanks for the warning!" Agnes replied

as Attie parked the silver bullet buggy a safe distance away. Not wanting to waste any time, she jumped out and ran over, clutching her map. "We're trying to find Diamond McGlinty's Garage. Can you point us in the right direction?"

The young man squinted at Agnes from behind his spectacles. "You're ... a *child*."

"That's right. My name's Agnes Gamble." She held out her hand.

"Hamish Cruthers," the young man replied, blinking as he shook it. He peered over at the silver bullet buggy. "Am I seeing things, or is that a *rat* driving your vehicle?"

Agnes winced, hoping Attie hadn't heard. He hated it when people mistook him for a rodent. "Actually, he's an elephant shrew." She knew it must appear odd for her and Attie to

be adventuring through the desert on their own, but with the hyrax pups' lives hanging in the balance, she didn't have time to explain. "I don't mean to be rude, but we're in a rush. If you could please just direct us to Diamond McGlinty's, we'll be on our way."

Hamish raised his eyebrows. "Why, of course."

As he inspected Agnes's map, she stole a glance under Hamish's tent, where a deep, dark hole the size and shape of Agnes's bedroom floor had been dug into the sand.

Something silver glinted in the shadows. Imagining it might be a piece of ancient treasure, Agnes shuffled closer to get a better look. All at once, she heard a strange beeping noise and a group of eight-legged metallic robots came scuttling out of the darkness. Despite being no bigger than chihuahuas, they each managed to carry a sealed wooden crate on their back.

"Don't be alarmed," Hamish Cruthers said jollily, as Agnes stepped back. "They're just my robotic assistants – spiderlings, I call them. They're stronger than me and make quick work of excavating a site like this."

Agnes could see where the robots got their name from. Like a spider, each body was formed of a long abdomen and a small, round head with a bank of glowing green eyes. As the spiderlings scurried past, Agnes saw they were loading their crates onto a truck parked behind the tent.

"The artefacts I've unearthed here are being delivered to a museum in America," Hamish explained. "I'm an Egyptologist, you see. I spend my time looking for ancient relics that I can send to institutions around the world, where they can be studied  and admired." He turned his attention back to Agnes's map and rubbed his chin. "Now, let me see... Diamond McGlinty's Garage is about here, so" – he shielded his eyes from the sun and pointed into the distance – "you'll need to drive in that direction for twenty kilometres or so to reach it."

"Thank you," Agnes said, gathering up her map. Quick as she could, she hotfooted it back to the silver bullet buggy, and she and Attie zoomed off.

Diamond McGlinty's Garage sat at the side of a long, empty road running through the desert. From the sleek design of the business card, Agnes had imagined the garage to be modern and smart-looking. Instead, it consisted of a wire-fenced yard filled with used cars, a rusty petrol pump and a small shop housed in a dilapidated tin building.

To avoid awkward questions, Agnes and Attie hid the silver bullet buggy behind a sandy mound and made their way over on foot. As they drew closer, Agnes's nose twitched. The air reeked of petrol and exhaust fumes – the same smells Attie had detected at the hyrax burrow. It had to be a sign they were in the right place.

Attie wiped his paw across the bonnet of a used car, leaving a clean line through the filth. "These haven't been cleaned in months," he observed, sticking his long tongue out in disapproval. "This garage can't do much business."

Agnes doubted many people passed this way at all. The area seemed deserted, like a forgotten corner of the world. It was the perfect place for a criminal to go unnoticed.

"Over there," Attie said, flattening his ears like he did whenever he sensed danger.

Sitting at either side of the shop's front door were two wolf-like creatures with long legs and pointed snouts. Their slender bodies were covered in rough, sand-coloured fur, except for a thick black strip over their spines. *Black-backed jackals.* Agnes understood why Attie was scared; jackals ate small mammals like him. "Climb onto my shoulder," she whispered. "You'll be safe if we pretend you're my pet."

"Your *pet*?" Attie put his hands on his hips. "You cannot be serious. The indignity of it!"

Agnes gave him a hard stare. "Can you think of a better idea?"

His expression softened. "Well ... no. Just don't tell any of the other agents. I'll never live it down."

The jackals gave a low growl as Agnes advanced with Attie on her shoulder. They wore jewelled collars with diamanté name tags around their necks. The jackal on the left was named Set; the one on the right was Sabra.

Set sniffed the air. "Smells like ..."

"... dinner," Sabra finished, licking her lips. They both slunk closer, gazing hungrily at Attie.

Agnes lifted her chin and strode past, pretending not to understand them.

The shop door opened with a creak. Inside, the air was stale and musty. A wobbling ceiling fan whirred overhead and a refrigerator hummed loudly in one corner. Agnes stood on her tiptoes to see over the maze of half-empty shelves. At the very back

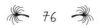

of the shop was a cashier's desk. A woman dressed in denim dungarees was sitting behind it, chewing gum. She had a side-parted Afro and wore heavy gold jewellery, including a diamanté necklace that matched Set and Sabra's collars. The pendant was shaped into a name: *DIAMOND*.

"Good afternoon," Diamond said, scrutinizing Agnes as she approached the desk. "What's a little girl like you doing out here on your own?"

"On my *own*?" Agnes repeated. "Oh no, I'm travelling with my uncle. He's sent me to get some ... lemonade." She didn't like lying, but Diamond McGlinty was a suspect and couldn't be trusted with the truth. "He found your business card near a hyrax burrow in the desert," she continued, pulling the card out of her pocket and holding it up. "How do you think it got there?"

Diamond narrowed her gaze. "How should I know?" She tapped a manicured nail against a box of business cards on the desk. "It could have been dropped by anyone who'd been in here."

The business card box was almost full, so Agnes doubted there had been many customers. It made her wonder how Diamond could afford all that jewellery...

Attie's fur tickled Agnes's neck as he whispered into her ear. "Behind the desk – look!"

Agnes angled her head and spied a half-eaten Peanut Paradiso next to the till. Before she could stop herself, she let out a gasp.

"Something wrong?" Diamond asked, leaning forward.

Agnes gulped. "No, nothing." She grabbed a couple of cans of lemonade and handed over a few Egyptian pound notes. "I'll take these. Keep the change." She made for the door without another word. Set and Sabra eyed her suspiciously as she stepped outside and hurried away.

When she and Attie were out of earshot, he hopped to the ground. "The Peanut Paradiso, the business card, the smell of exhaust fumes – they all point to Diamond being at the hyrax burrow. She must be involved with the hyrax pups' disappearance!"

"The evidence adds up," Agnes agreed. "But if Diamond has abducted *all* the animals the Commander told us about, then where can she be keeping them? There isn't room

for a baby elephant in that shop."

Attie stroked his whiskers. "Good point. She must be holding them somewhere else. Let's wait till nightfall and stake-out the garage. Diamond will have to leave at some point and when she does, we'll follow her."

Back at the garage shop, Diamond McGlinty sloped across to the window to watch her last customer, a young girl with a pet elephant shrew, hurry away across the yard. The girl's shifty behaviour had left Diamond uneasy. "I know when I'm being lied to," Diamond muttered as the shop door creaked open and her two pet jackals prowled inside.

"Grrr," said Sabra.

"Yoooowl," said Set.

"Exactly." Diamond tossed a fresh piece of gum into her mouth and started chewing. "I want you to keep an eye out for that kid and tell me if she comes snooping around here again. I'd bet my diamonds she's up to something."

CHAPTER FIVE

It was early evening and the light was fading. Perched at the top of a rocky hill overlooking Diamond McGlinty's Garage, Agnes adjusted the hairy sleeves of her adult aardwolf costume. There was no telling how long this stake-out would take, so she needed to be comfortable.

"Aardwolves are frequently seen in this area," Attie said, padding closer in his aardwolf-cub disguise. Every part of him – from his long whiskers to his tail – was hidden. "If Diamond or one of her jackals spots us, they shouldn't pay us any attention."

Agnes had never met a real aardwolf, but she'd read all about them. They looked like small, slender hyenas with yellow-and-black striped fur and distinctive manes running along their spines. They were also nocturnal, which meant they were most active at night.

"You'd better make sure nobody notices you eating that then," she told him, pointing to the pumpkin-seed-and-fried-banana sandwich he was holding. "I know successful stake-outs require snacks, but aardwolves eat *termites*."

Through the costume's eyeholes, Attie blinked. "I hadn't thought about that." With a huff, he opened a secret pouch in the tail of his costume and stuffed the sandwich out of sight.

Agnes was glad her costume was thick and furry as the air had grown chilly. It was strange to think of deserts as cold places, but when night fell, temperatures could drop below freezing. She watched Diamond McGlinty down at the garage, shutting up for the night – switching off the lights in her shop and locking the front door. Her two jackals skulked around the used-car yard, sniffing the ground. Diamond whistled them over as she climbed into the driver's seat of a battered red pick-up truck. There were two luxury jackal-beds fixed in the back.

"Let's return to the silver bullet buggy," Attie said. "We've got to be ready to follow her."

But Agnes's attention had been captured by something else. A small dark shape was flitting in and out of the shadows underneath the used cars. It reminded her of the mirage she'd seen at the Flower's shrews' burrow... Except now she wasn't so sure that *had* been a mirage.

She reached for the aviascope (the only item of equipment she hadn't left in the silver bullet buggy) and fitted the "owl" lens. Like aardwolves, owls were nocturnal creatures, and had specially adapted eyesight to see in the dark.

Through the lens, everything appeared bathed in daylight. As the dark shape came into focus, Agnes frowned. It was a four-legged animal with a bushy tail and large ears. She had no idea what colour it was because it was dressed in a tight-fitting all-black ninja suit, with a small rucksack on its back and a mask covering much of its face.

The only animals she knew who wore clothes and kit were those that worked for **SPEARS** ... or the known *enemies* of **SPEARS**.

Her mind swirled with questions as she tucked the aviascope away. Was this mystery animal another of Diamond's pets? Could it be involved in the hyrax pups' disappearance?

All of a sudden, Attie started shouting: "Unhand me this instant!"

Before Agnes knew what was happening, a sack was thrown over her head and everything went dark.

"Get off!" she yelled, kicking. But the arms that gripped her were too strong. She was lifted into the air and flung onto a hard surface. "Attie! Attie, are you there?"

There was no response. As an engine rumbled into life beneath her, Agnes peered through the eyeholes of her costume. All she could see was the inside of a hessian sack – the same material as the scrap she and Attie had discovered at the hyrax burrow. With an icy chill, she realized what must have happened: she and Attie had been mistaken for *real* aardwolves and abducted by the very criminal they'd been searching for!

Her pulse was racing but she tried to stay calm and breathe deeply. There had to be a way for her to break free and find her partner. Together, they might be able to turn this situation to their advantage by apprehending the kidnapper and forcing them to reveal the location of the missing hyrax pups.

As the vehicle clattered over bumpy terrain, Agnes listened out for clues. She could hear the scratch of claws, ruffle of feathers and wheezy snorts of other creatures who must have been loaded onto the vehicle alongside her. But however hard she concentrated, she couldn't hear Attie. What if he was hurt?

They travelled for what felt like hours. Agnes paid attention to the crackle of gravel under the vehicle's tyres, wondering where they were being taken. It had to be somewhere in the desert because there was no other traffic around. At one point, she tried to wriggle free from the sack so she could use her aviascope, but the hessian was tied too tightly.

Eventually, the truck came to an abrupt

stop and Agnes was carried into somewhere cool and echoey – a tunnel, she guessed. Her aardwolf costume cushioned her landing as she fell onto something rough and prickly that smelled like fresh straw.

Without warning, the sack was ripped off and light returned to her eyes.

She found herself squinting through the thick metal bars of a cage, overlooking a candlelit chamber with hewn stone walls. Her mysterious captor was nowhere to be seen, but scattered across the dusty floor were other cages. In one, a plump North African ostrich was pecking furiously at its bars; in another a weary-looking leopard paced up and down; and a full-grown rhinoceros was slumped on the floor of a reinforced enclosure. Agnes searched for

the hyrax pups but couldn't find them.

A lump formed at the back of her throat as she gazed at the captive wild animals. She imagined how confused and scared they must all be, and felt anger rise inside her like boiling water. She didn't understand how anyone could be so cruel.

No matter what, she *had* to free them.
All of them.

As she sprang out of her aardwolf
costume, she heard a gasp from behind her.

"I don't believe it," exclaimed a croaky
voice. "You're from **SPEARS**!"

CHAPTER SIX

Agnes spun around. The croaky voice belonged to a tiny tortoise with a mottled pale-gold and brown shell. It had to be an Egyptian tortoise, the smallest tortoise in the Northern Hemisphere.

"What are the chances?" the reptile muttered excitedly. "My name's Rameses and I'm a retired **SPEARS** agent!"

"Really?" Agnes could barely believe her good fortune. If Rameses had been trained as an agent, he'd have all kinds of special skills that might come in useful to help everyone escape. "I'm Agnes. My partner, Attie, was disguised as an aardwolf cub when we were captured. Do you have any idea where he might be?"

Rameses trotted to Agnes's side and poked his head through the cage bars. "I was brought here two days ago and I haven't seen any cubs or infants."

The poacher must be holding them in a different place, Agnes thought. That would explain why the hyrax pups weren't there.

With any luck, Attie had found them and was keeping them safe. She wished she still had her chromaphone on her so she could talk to him.

"Those are the only exits?" she asked Rameses, counting the openings to four dark tunnels in the chamber walls. There was a different animal painted above each one in the style of hieroglyphics, the ancient Egyptian writing. She remembered Hamish

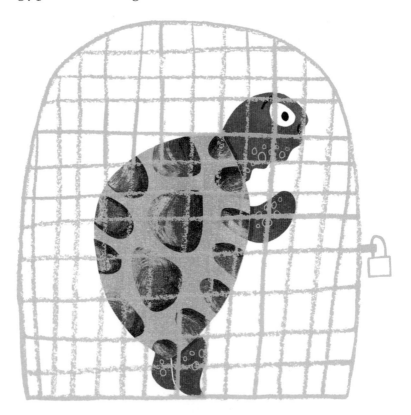

Cruthers mentioning that there were ancient tombs hidden in the desert; this chamber must be part of one.

"That's right," Rameses said as Agnes slipped her hand through the cage bars and rattled the padlock attached to the door. "Is Phil still ruling the roost at **SPEARS**?"

"Yes, he's our Commander," she answered. With the right tools she might be able to pick the padlock open, but they were all back in the silver bullet buggy. "He organized a mission to investigate this recent surge of animal trafficking in Africa. I don't suppose you've identified who is behind it, have you?"

Rameses hung his head. "I'm afraid not. My glasses fell off when I was snatched and I'm terribly short-sighted without them. Beyond this cage, everything is *very* blurry."

"Not to worry," Agnes told him, smiling sympathetically. "Let's just concentrate on breaking out of here."

Changing to the "eagle" lens on the aviascope, she scanned the chamber, searching for anything she might use to help her break out. Between the cages stood

several wooden crates, a few bales of straw and some boxes of bottled water.

"You know, there's something familiar about your face," Rameses murmured. "I just can't quite put my shell on it."

As Agnes swept the aviascope over the floor, she spied a glimmering line of transparent yellow pharaoh ants. They were one of the most successful insect species on the planet, found in almost every country in the world. "Hello there!" she hollered, waving madly at the marching line. "I work for **SPEARS**. Can you help me?"

For a moment, she thought the ants hadn't heard her. Then the column made an abrupt ninety-degree turn and wound its way over the stone slabs towards her cage. There was a soft *click* as they all stood to attention.

Agnes had never spoken to an ant before so it took her by surprise when the whole procession spoke as one.

"**SPEARS** is our ally," the ants said in a strange, humming voice. "**SPEARS** is trapped?"

Not for the first time, she felt thankful to be part of an organization with such a good reputation among the animal kingdom. "Unfortunately, yes. Could you help me pick this lock?"

The ants formed a circle, murmuring to each other. "We agree," they said, eventually. "Two hundred and forty seconds."

In one unbroken line, they raced up the side of Agnes's cage and disappeared inside the padlock. Precisely four minutes later, there was a dull clunk and the padlock sprang loose.

"It worked!" Rameses cheered.

Agnes's spirits lifted. So far, so good. All she needed to do now was find Attie and the kidnapped babies. She thanked the pharaoh ants, who saluted and marched away to open the padlocks of the other cages. Soon, the chamber was bustling with activity.

"Freedom!" the leopard roared, swinging its long tail. The rhino got to its feet and barrelled out of its enclosure, narrowly missing Rameses, who was steadily plodding across the floor.

"Which way? Which way?" the ostrich fretted, shaking its bushy black feathers as it whizzed between the four tunnel openings.

Agnes knew it was her job to lead everyone to safety, but she still wasn't sure which tunnel to take. If she chose the wrong one, she might lead the group deeper into the tomb and risk getting lost. Doing her best Commander Phil impression, she climbed onto an empty cage and cleared her throat.

"Everyone, I need your attention!"

The rhino twitched its ears and turned its horns towards her. The leopard and the ostrich fell silent.

"I understand you might be feeling panicked," Agnes said, "but please try to remain calm. I'm a **SPEARS** agent and I'm going to get us all out of here." She bent down

to Rameses and whispered,
"I could use your help. There's
a different animal hieroglyph above
each of the exits. If we're really in an ancient
Egyptian tomb, they might give us a clue
about which passage we should take."

Rameses squinted up at the wall. "What
do they look like?"

"Well, this one is a bird with a curved
beak and long feathers at the back of its
head," Agnes explained. "A pelican, maybe."

He appeared to chew the information
over. "We'd better not go that way. The ancient
Egyptians associated pelicans with death."

Agnes shivered and quickly described
the other three animals. There was a
baboon standing on two legs, a dung
beetle holding a ball of dung and

a regal-looking jackal that reminded her unnervingly of Diamond McGlinty's pets. Rameses considered each symbol carefully and finally came to a stop by the dung-beetle passage. "All of these animals symbolize death in Egyptian mythology, but the dung beetle – the scarab – also signifies the rising sun. My best guess is it's this way."

Staring into the shadowy tunnel, Agnes's skin prickled. The stone walls were painted with so many dung beetles it looked like the ancient Egyptians had decorated it in scarab wallpaper. She clenched her fists. Afraid that time was running out, she had no choice.

They would all have to risk it.

CHAPTER SEVEN

The large tunnel was dark and full of cobwebs. Agnes's palms sweated as she guided the animals along using the "owl" lens on the aviascope to help her see in the gloom. To avoid stumbling into each other, she had told everyone to hold the tail of the creature in front, creating an animal chain.

"You're doing an excellent job," Rameses commented, tucked inside Agnes's top pocket with his head and front legs hanging out. The arrangement had been his suggestion, to help save time. "Just keep going. We're bound to see daylight soon."

Agnes appreciated Rameses's optimism, but with every step she grew more worried that she'd chosen the wrong path. The animals were all relying on her and after what they'd been through, she didn't want to let them down.

The ostrich – who had introduced herself as Tara – started squawking: "Look! Look! There's light ahead!"

Agnes lowered the aviascope, hoping

to see a beam of sunshine piercing the darkness. Instead, a tiny candle flickered in the murk. "Stay quiet everyone," she cautioned. "There could be someone else here."

"And be careful where you tread," Rameses added in a whisper. "Especially you, Anika."

The rhino grunted.

As they crept towards the candle, its light revealed the opening to another chamber. The leopard, Zane, pricked up his ears and growled, "I can't hear anything yet..."

While the animals waited with their backs pressed against the tunnel wall, Agnes summoned up the courage to venture inside. Her heart thudded as she slid around the corner ...

... but there
was no one there.

"It's safe," she
told the others
with a sigh.
"Follow me."

One by
one, the party
emerged into a
chamber larger
than the last.
The floor was
cluttered with
empty cages,
and a canopy of
hessian sacks
dangled from
the ceiling.

Agnes scowled as she cast her gaze over the various traps and snares hanging on the walls. *Poaching equipment.*

A desk stood in one corner. Agnes warned the others not to touch anything while she and Rameses went over to investigate.

Hidden under a pile of maps, she discovered a leather notebook and a small plastic lunchbox. The notebook contained a list of international names and addresses – illegal animal buyers, she guessed. Inside the lunchbox she found a mouldy apple core and the remnants of a Peanut Paradiso. "This *has* to be where the animal trader works," she told Rameses, explaining the three clues that she and Attie had found outside the hyrax burrow. "Whoever they are, they're using these tombs as their base of operations." She ripped out the contacts page and stuffed it in her pocket. Hopefully, Commander Phil would get a look at it later.

"What's that down there?" Rameses asked, pointing his head under the desk. "I can't quite see."

Agnes crouched to get a better view. A small stone pedal protruded from the floor, worn in the centre from where it had been repeatedly pushed. Curious, she gave it a press.

All at once, the floor shuddered and a deep groan resounded in the walls. "What's happening?" Tara asked, twisting her long pink neck in all directions.

Anika snorted and stomped her foot. "There!" she boomed.

A large circular hole had opened in the far wall. Beyond it was another chamber filled with more poaching equipment and a handful of animal cages. This time, two of them were *full*.

"The babies!" Rameses exclaimed, jumping up and down in Agnes's pocket.

"We've found them!"

Agnes rushed through the opening
and spotted the three hyrax pups huddled
together in the corner of a cage. Their long
black whiskers were trembling. "Everything's
going to be OK," she said gently, kneeling to
inspect their padlock. "You're safe now. I'm
going to return you to your parents."

One of the hyrax pups lifted its head and wriggled its button nose. "To Mummy and Daddy?" it asked hopefully.

"That's right," Agnes promised. "Don't worry." She did a double take when she noticed that the padlock was already open. *But how...?*

"Agnes!" called a familiar voice from the other side of the cavern. "You're all right!" Attie was stood beside an enclosure of wiry-haired warthog piglets, trying to use a rusty old paperclip to pick their padlock.

"Attie!" She ran over and hugged him.

"Don't fuss, don't fuss," he insisted, although Agnes caught him smiling at the corners of his mouth. "Did you get a glimpse of whoever snatched us?"

"No, and neither did any of my new friends." She swiftly introduced Rameses in her top pocket, followed by Tara, Zane and Anika. "We think we've found a way out – a tunnel painted with dung beetles."

Attie crinkled his nose. "I don't like the sound of that, but good work. We'd better get going." The cage door creaked open, and the warthog piglets came stampeding out, squealing.

"Stay calm, little ones!" Tara cried as they dashed between her long pink legs.

A line of concern formed on Attie's brow.

"We can't have them running wild in an ancient tomb like this; there could be all kinds of hazards! We need to find a way to keep them safe while we get out of here."

Glancing at some hessian sacks lying about the chamber, Agnes had a brainwave. "I've got an idea. Do you think you can construct a few slings from that hessian, Attie?"

Once the slings were complete, the adult animals were buddied up with a number of infants. Tara carried the three hyrax pups in a sling around the base of her neck; Zane had two piglets strapped to his back and the rest of the litter were fastened to Anika's huge leathery rump. Agnes continued to carry

Rameses in her pocket, while Attie scurried here and there, checking that the infants were secure.

"All right, everyone," Agnes said, venturing out into the dung-beetle tunnel. "Remember: keep hold of the tail in front."

They fumbled slowly through the darkness. The tunnel seemed to go on for ever, but Agnes felt a renewed sense of strength with Attie at her side. She had half expected him to recognize Rameses, but then lots of agents must have worked for **SPEARS** over the years and Attie couldn't be expected to know them all.

Eventually, a chorus of roaring, honking and grunting echoed around the walls as daylight was spotted up ahead. Agnes stowed away her aviascope and led the others into a large room with a patterned floor made of green, red, blue, yellow, white and black tiles. A set of steps on the far side climbed towards a slice of orange-blue sky. The sun was dawning, which meant Agnes and Attie had been underground all night.

"Hooray!" Anika bellowed, sounding like a foghorn. "We made it!"

Agnes's chest emptied with relief as she took a step forward.

"Wait!" Attie snapped.

But he was too late. The red tile under Agnes's foot crumbled to dust, leaving her wobbling one-legged over a hole in the floor. "Woah!" she cried, recovering her balance just in time. "What happened?"

Attie peered over the edge. "There's a pit below us. The floor must be booby-trapped."

"There must be a safe way to cross," Rameses said, studying the coloured tiles. "Maybe there's a pattern to it, like some sort of colour code?"

Agnes scoured the room for clues. The walls were carved with the hieroglyphs of

five different animals – a horned viper,
a hummingbird, a hooded cobra and a
woodpecker. The fifth animal was either a
pigeon or a dove, she wasn't sure.

"Perhaps it has something to do with
the colour of the animals?" Attie proposed.
"Horned vipers are sand-coloured, so that
could mean yellow—"

But when he placed his foot on the
nearest yellow tile, it collapsed from under
him, and Agnes had to grab his tail to stop
him from falling through.

"That can't be right," she decided.
"Anyway, hummingbirds are multicoloured,
so it wouldn't make sense." She considered
the carved animals carefully. There had to be
some connection between them. The sound

of her footsteps echoed as she paced up and down, brainstorming with Attie. They both had lots of ideas, but none seemed to fit. After thirty minutes, Agnes had almost given up hope of finding the answer when one of the warthog piglets squeaked, giving her a brainwave. "That's it!" she realized. "That's what they all have in common – it's to do with their young. They all lay white eggs!"

"So then, the answer is *white*?" Rameses asked.

"Let's find out," Agnes replied. She reached out with her toes and tapped the nearest white square. To her amazement, it didn't crumble. She hopped over and tried another white square, then another and another.

"Agnes, you've cracked it!" Attie cried.

"Only tread on the white squares – all the other colours are booby-trapped," he told everyone. "And be careful."

Taking it slow and steady, the group stepped carefully from white tile to white tile. They made it halfway across the floor before a shadow drew over them. Agnes looked up to see the silhouette of a three-headed figure blocking the exit...

Diamond McGlinty and her two jackals. It had to be.

CHAPTER EIGHT

The silhouette separated into distinct figures, but they weren't who Agnes had been expecting. *"Hamish Cruthers!"* she exclaimed.

She was so flabbergasted she staggered backwards and almost fell through a blue floor tile.

Cruthers, who was clutching an empty hessian sack, was accompanied by four of his green-eyed spiderlings. His linen shirt and shorts were gone, replaced by a stylish claret suit and pinstriped cravat. "The little girl who asked for directions?" he uttered. "What are *you* doing here?"

"What is *she* doing?" Attie responded, puffing out his chest. "What are *you* doing, more like? You're not an Egyptologist at all, are you? You're an illegal animal trader!"

As the clues slotted into place, Agnes couldn't believe she'd missed them before. Hamish Cruthers had known exactly where Diamond McGlinty's garage was; he must have picked up Diamond's business card and a Peanut Paradiso on his last visit. With a horrible sinking feeling, she remembered the crates she'd seen being loaded onto Cruthers' truck and realized they'd probably been full of animals. He must have been using the underground tombs to store the creatures while he organized buyers for them.

"I am a successful businessman," Hamish retorted, turning his nose up at

Attie. "And I will *not* be spoken to like that by a rat."

"A *rat?*" Attie's fur stood on end. "How dare you!" Sensing a fight might ensue, Agnes scanned the floor and tried to memorize the positions of the white tiles. She and Attie were at a major disadvantage if they wanted to apprehend Cruthers. One false step, and they'd fall into the pit below. "And to think, we thought Diamond McGlinty was behind all this!" she remarked, stalling for time.

"The garage owner?" Cruthers snorted. "You must be joking. She couldn't build an empire like mine. It takes an exceptional amount of ingenuity to keep things running smoothly. I'd like to see Diamond McGlinty programme a fleet of spiderlings to do her bidding."

The spiderlings – of course. Agnes recalled the impossibly strong grip of her kidnapper and knew at once that it must have been one of Cruthers' robots. That was how he was operating – using the spiderlings as poachers.

"Well, your cruel scheme ends here!" Attie proclaimed. "In the name of **SPEARS**, I'm placing you under arrest for the illegal poaching and trading of some of Africa's rarest animals!"

Hamish laughed. "Oh, *please*. **SPEARS** can't stop me." He signalled over Attie's shoulder to where Tara, Anika and Zane were retreating across the white tiles. "Spiderlings, get those three back in their cages and see to it that the **SPEARS** agents are *permanently* deleted."

The spiderlings' eyes flashed red as they turned in the direction of the fleeing animals.

"Not so fast!" Attie declared. Quick as a flash, he hopped over several coloured tiles, barely touching them, and landed on a white one. The coloured tiles collapsed, creating a wide chasm in the floor.

For a split second, Agnes thought that the spiderlings wouldn't be able to reach them, but the robots promptly launched grappling hooks from their abdomens, which fixed to the ceiling so the machines could swing themselves across.

"Looks like it's going to be a glorious day," Cruthers said, grinning. "Pity you'll never see it." With a flamboyant flip of his suit jacket, he spun around and disappeared outside.

"Now what?" Agnes asked as the spiderlings advanced. She and Attie had been trained in the secret fighting style

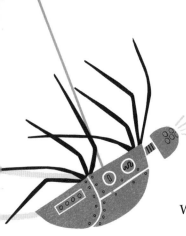

of animai-tai but it was
almost impossible to
defend themselves when they
were so heavily outnumbered.

"I'm thinking!" Attie said,
inching backwards.

Agnes felt Rameses trembling in her
pocket. She thought of asking the larger
animals for help, but they were shielding the
terrified infants. Out of the corner of her eye,
she spotted a shadowy figure dart across the
ceiling. There was a loud *swish* as it came
hurtling through the air and pounced on
one of the spiderlings, knocking the robot
off its eight feet. More coloured tiles
disintegrated as the spiderling tumbled
across the floor and clattered through a
hole into the pit below.

It happened so fast it took Agnes a moment to remember that she'd seen that shadowy figure before. It was the same bushy-tailed animal wearing a black ninja suit that she'd spotted at Diamond McGlinty's Garage and the Flower's shrews' burrow. It must have been following them.

Beeping madly, the remaining three spiderlings jerked forward. A pair of razor-sharp pincers appeared from a slot in each of their heads and started snapping through the air.

Click. Click. Click.

One of the spiderlings made for Attie; another turned on Agnes. Cold sweat beaded her forehead as she stumbled away. The floor was full of holes now;

one wrong step and she'd find herself
buried beneath the ancient tomb.

"Try a soaring-eagle kick!"
the ninja called across to them.

Agnes wasn't sure
how it knew animai-tai,
but the soaring-eagle kick
was a good suggestion.

She and Attie bent their knees, stretched their arms above their heads and then dragged them down very fast. The momentum launched them into the air at exactly the same moment, so they looked like a pair of synchronized acrobats.

Agnes came down feet first. Her desert boots collided with the spiderling's body with a thundering *CLANG!* The robot scrambled to stay upright but eventually fell onto a red tile, which turned to dust beneath it. At the same moment, the remaining two spiderlings crashed through the floor, dispensed by Attie and the ninja.

"You two made quick work of those metal monsters," the ninja commented, pulling off its hood and mask. Two enormous cream-coloured ears popped out, along with a

pointed snout and small black nose. *A fennec fox!* Agnes had never met one before but knew they were the smallest foxes in the

world – a desert-dwelling species that used its oversized ears to keep it cool in the heat.

"*Marceline?*" Rameses said, wriggling in Agnes's pocket. "It that you?"

Agnes lifted the tortoise out and placed him on the floor. "Do you two know each other?"

"We're best friends!" Rameses replied. "We trained together at **SPEARS**."

That explains Marceline's outfit, Agnes thought. The fox probably had disguises left over from her agent days.

"When I heard Rameses had been abducted, I began trying to track him," Marceline explained. She nudged Rameses' shell with her snout. "A **SPEARS** agent never forgets, eh, old friend?"

"Thank you so much for your help,"

Agnes said. "I'm Agent Gamble and this is my partner, Agent Attenborough."

"Agent *Gamble*?" Marceline trotted closer, scrutinizing Agnes's face. "I don't believe it!" She gathered Rameses in her jaws and lifted him up. "Can't you see the resemblance, Rameses? This is Ranulph and Azalea's daughter!"

"Well, I'll be...!" Rameses exclaimed. "I *thought* your face was familiar. Your mother, Azalea, was my **SPEARS** partner."

"And your father, Ranulph, was mine," Marceline said.

"*What?*" Agnes's voice was frail. She felt as if her legs might crumble like one of the coloured floor tiles.

"I'm so sorry to interrupt," Attie said, his tail and whiskers twitching, "but ... Hamish Cruthers is getting away!"

CHAPTER NINE

As Agnes sprinted up
the steps and out of the tomb,
she felt her brain would burst with
all the questions she wanted to ask

 140

Rameses and Marceline. Her heart soared as she imagined the stories they might be able to tell her about her parents...

But she needed to put all that to the back of her mind and focus. She and Attie had a mission to complete.

As they surfaced, she recognized her surroundings immediately. They had emerged from the large hole at the supposed archaeological site where she'd first met Hamish Cruthers. His truck was gone, but the table of digging tools and canvas tent were still there.

"Over here," Attie said, running past a set of tyre tracks in the sand. "Cruthers must have gone this way."

Agnes used the "American woodcock" lens on the aviascope to search in all directions. "He's heading north," she said, spotting his truck in the distance. "But without the silver bullet buggy we'll never catch him."

There was a commotion behind them as the other animals clambered out of the hole. Anika stomped through the sand, snorting with glee; Zane did an enormous feline stretch and flexed his claws. Rameses and Marceline quickly got to work untying the hyrax pups and piglets, who fell about and started playing.

As Tara shook out her wings, Agnes remembered something: North African ostriches were the fastest land birds in the world. "Tara, do you think you're strong enough to chase after Cruthers with me on your back?"

The ostrich batted her eyelashes. "You bet I am. Jump on up."

"You'll have to go on your own, Agnes," Attie warned. "I need to grab my chromaphone from the silver bullet buggy near Diamond McGlinty's garage, and contact **SPEARS** in order to return these babies to their parents."

"I'll accompany her," Marceline offered, leaping into Agnes's lap. "Rameses – you can help Agent Attenborough with the others."

With no time to spare, Tara pointed her

beak in the direction of the desert road and
they set off. Agnes clung to Tara's feathers
as the ostrich's feet pounded the dry earth,
sending Agnes and Marceline juddering and
jerking with every step.

Cruthers' truck soon appeared in the
distance, a cloud of dust around its back
wheels. Agnes wondered if the crates
she'd seen loaded onto it yesterday were

still on board. If so, the animals inside would
be hungry and dehydrated. She needed to get
them out as soon as possible.

As the growl of the engine grew louder,
Agnes called into Tara's ear. "Can you run
alongside the truck, so Marceline and I can
jump across?"

Clenching her beak, Tara accelerated until
she was only a metre away. "Now!" she squawked.

Agnes and Marceline made the leap at the same time. Agnes caught hold of a length of strapping on the truck's roof and managed to latch on; Marceline dug in with her claws and teeth. In the wing mirror, Agnes caught sight of Hamish Cruthers' reflection. Red-faced and sweaty, he was glaring right at them! With a snarl, he yanked on the steering wheel.

"He's trying to shake us off!" Marceline yelled.

"We could use the coconut-crab pinch to hold on!" Agnes suggested, remembering the manoeuvre from her animai-tai training. Coconut crabs had the strongest grip in the animal kingdom; it should keep them steady.

"Good idea!" Marceline shouted back. "Your mother was brilliant at that one!"

As the vehicle veered left and right, Agnes moved her hands and feet into the correct positions and crab-crawled up to the roof, clinging on tightly. She felt a tremor as the truck rolled from sand onto tarmac. Cruthers had made it to the desert road.

Marceline's huge ears flapped in the wind. "Careful, he's speeding up!"

Agnes tried to shuffle closer to the driver's cab, but with the increased air pressure it felt like she was pushing against bricks.

Suddenly, she heard Cruthers shouting: "Argh!"

The brakes squealed as the truck came to an abrupt halt, and only their coconut-crab pinch saved them from flying off into the scorched desert air. Agnes sprang to her feet on top of the truck as Cruthers leaned out of the driver's-side window, shaking his fist.

"What are you *doing* there?" he barked. "Move!"

Ahead of him, standing coolly with her arms folded in the middle of the road, was Diamond McGlinty.

"I don't think so, pal!"

To Agnes's surprise, the garage owner

and her two jackals had formed a barricade of filthy used cars right across the tarmac road.

Marceline waved. "Diamond!"

"You know her?" Agnes asked.

"I met her a few hours ago. She told me about you and Attie – that's how I tracked you and Rameses to the underground tomb." Marceline nodded at Set and Sabra, the jackals. "Diamond's an animal lover. After I revealed what Cruthers was up to, she wanted to help."

Heat rose to Agnes's cheeks as she realized how foolish she'd been. She should never have jumped to conclusions about Diamond.

"If you won't move out of the way, then I will make you," Cruthers snarled, revving the engine.

Marceline stiffened. "We've got to stop him!"

Agnes could only think of one thing that might help. As quickly as possible, she scrambled down from the truck, grabbed a sharp stone from the side of the road and jabbed it into one of the truck's tyres. The air escaped with a low hiss.

"That was your final warning, McGlinty," Cruthers announced, scowling. With a roar of the engine, the truck shot forward, swerved on the flat tyre and drove straight into a sandbank at the road's edge.

Diamond laughed as she strolled over. "You were saying, Cruthers?" She winked at Agnes and Marceline. "Don't worry, my jackals and I will keep an eye on him while you check out the back of the truck."

With Marceline's help, Agnes lifted the tarpaulin and found several crates of very hot and very relieved African animals. Among them were six leopard cubs, three rhino calves and a baby elephant – all the infants Commander Phil had mentioned during his emergency meeting. And now they were safe.

CHAPTER TEN

Agnes got a fluttery feeling in her stomach
as her chromaphone started vibrating. She
crouched down and peered inside the dark

entrance to the Flower's shrews' burrow. "Attie, Commander Phil is calling."

"I'll be right there," Attie replied. He made a scratchy noise as he scurried out, his whiskers dusted with sand. "You'd better answer promptly. We can't keep the Commander waiting."

Agnes took a deep breath to steady her nerves. She always felt anxious after the Commander read one of their mission reports – it detailed everything that had gone right, and everything that had gone *wrong* during their operation. She flicked a switch on the chromaphone and the rippling rainbow-coloured surface transformed into a video image.

"Agent Gamble, Agent Attenborough, glad to see you're both safe and well," Commander

Phil said sternly. He was sitting at his desk in **SPEARS** HQ surrounded by several piles of the same book, with a red spine and black

lettering. "I understand your time in Egypt has been eventful – kidnapping, booby traps, a high-speed ostrich chase...?"

Attie cleared his throat. "We were certainly kept busy, sir."

"I thought you'd like to know," the Commander continued, "that thanks to the information you recovered from Hamish Cruthers' notebook, we've been able to trace all the buyers in his criminal network. Needless to say, they will soon be behind bars." He grabbed a copy of the red-spined book from beside him and flicked it open to a particular page. It showed a sour-faced photo of Hamish Cruthers dressed in a scruffy grey prison uniform. "I've had Cruthers' mugshot added to this latest edition of the **SPEARS** *Handbook of Known*

Enemies. Future agents can read about how he masqueraded as an Egyptologist; hopefully, they won't fall for any similar tricks."

Agnes gazed into her lap, feeling guilty. If only she'd seen through Cruthers' disguise, she and Attie would have rescued all those animals sooner. "We're sorry we let him outwit us. We both thought the clues pointed to another suspect."

"Investigations are rarely straightforward," the Commander said. "The important thing is to learn from your experiences and grow into a better agent. What lessons will you take away from this?"

"Not to jump to conclusions," Attie said gloomily.

Agnes considered the question carefully. The mission, she knew, wouldn't have been successful without help from Diamond, Rameses and Marceline. "I've learned that you can find friends in the most unexpected of places," she said. "You just have to look hard enough."

Phil's beak split into a wide smile. "That's certainly right! Congratulations, both of you."

Later that evening, Agnes, Attie, Rameses and Marceline were sat around a campfire just outside the Flower's shrews' burrow. "Toasted pumpkin-seed-and-fried-banana kebab?" Attie offered, passing around a plate of his favourite sandwiches mounted on sticks.

They smelled delicious, but Agnes was too excited to eat at the moment. She leaned forward, listening intently to Rameses and Marceline.

"Your parents decided to retire from **SPEARS** when they had you," Marceline explained. "They thought it would be too dangerous to bring you along on missions."

"And they were right," Rameses said. "You were a baby! But now look – you've grown into a fine young lady and a brilliant **SPEARS** agent. They would be so proud of you."

"*We're* so proud of you," Marceline added.

Agnes's eyes welled up with emotion. Attie snuggled next to her.

"Here, we have a gift for you," Marceline said, pulling something out from her rucksack. It was a photo album, covered in a hand-painted tapioca-leaf pattern in the exact style of Agnes's bedroom wallpaper in her old house.

Agnes gasped as she opened it. Illuminated in the firelight were photos of her mum and dad wearing **SPEARS** uniforms just like hers. They appeared abseiling down mountains, rafting on fast-flowing rivers or trekking through thick jungle. Marceline and Rameses were there too. "Thank you," she breathed. "This is amazing." With a twinge of sadness, she

remembered that she and Attie had to return home tomorrow. "Do you think I could see you again? I'd love to hear more about my parents' adventures."

"See us again?" Marceline laughed, flashing her pointed teeth. "Agnes, now that we're in your life, you're never getting rid of us!"

"You can consider us your honorary aunt and uncle," Rameses said. "I hope we're not too embarrassing."

Agnes giggled. "You haven't met my uncle Douglas."

OPERATION: SANDWHISKERS

by Agnes Gamble (**SPEARS** Field Agent)

UPDATE:

Operation Sandwhiskers has been a mission full of surprises. Despite being kidnapped by poachers (who we later discovered were robots), Agent Attenborough and I managed to rescue lots of rare species and helped reunite animal families with their missing children. The best surprise of all was that I got to meet two retired **SPEARS** agents who used to be my parents' partners! Nothing can ever bring my mum and dad back, but with Rameses and Marceline in my life now, it feels like a small part of them has returned.

OBSERVATIONS:

* Pharaoh ants can be lifesavers.

* Never underestimate a tortoise.

* Pumpkin-seed-and-fried-banana
  sandwiches are much tastier when
  roasted over an open fire.

SPEARS HQ
FLUFFY-FACE CAT FOOD
TOWER, BIG GREY CITY

OPERATION: SANDWHISKERS

MISSION TYPE:	SEARCH & PROTECT
SPECIES NAME:	HYRAX PUPS

PROCAVIA CAPENSIS (SCIENTIFIC)

ASSIGNED EQUIPMENT:

AVIASCOPE, PEREGRINE
DRONE, SILVER BULLET
BUGGY,CHROMAPHONE

SECURITY CLASSIFICATION:

TOP SECRET

AGENT ATTENBOROUGH AND AGENT GAMBLE TO BE DEPLOYED
TO THE EASTERN DESERT FOR OPERATION: SANDWHISKERS

CASE FILE NUMBER: 03112018421

SPEARS OFFICIAL

COMMUNICATION

Dear Reader,

It's Commander Phil here, calling all **SPEARS** agents!

I'm proud to say that Agents Attenborough and Gamble have completed another successful mission for SPEARS and stopped an illegal animal trader from exploiting wild animals in Africa. Sadly, wildlife crime is still the biggest direct threat to the future of many of the world's most threatened species and more work needs to be done to eradicate it.

What's the problem?

Every year, millions of plants and animals are taken from the wild to be sold on as food, medicine, pets and materials. A large proportion of this trade is *illegal* and is threatening the survival of many endangered species. This trade not only has a devastating impact on plants, animals and ecosystems, but also on local communities. It fuels corruption, undermines development and creates instability in some of the world's poorest countries.

WHO'S IN DANGER?

Around 7000 species of animals are traded illegally around the world, from jaguars in South America, to rhinos in Africa and tigers in Asia. It's not just mammals that are under threat; countless species of fish, insects, birds and reptiles are also being over-exploited.

CRITICALLY ENDANGERED

AFRICAN ELEPHANT

The largest land mammals on earth, they can live for up to 70 years. An elephant's trunk contains over 40,000 muscles. Their ivory tusks are used to make jewellery and furniture.

Pangolins use their long, sticky tongues to help them eat ants and termites. They are covered in hard scales made of keratin – the same protein that human hair and nails are made of. Their scales are used in traditional medicine.

PANGOLIN

Despite their huge size and weight, black rhinos can run up to 34 miles per hour! Their hooked upper lips help them graze on leaves, roots and tree stems. They are poached for their horns, which are used in traditional medicine.

BLACK RHINO

These big cats are brilliant swimmers and use their long tails to help them balance when climbing trees.

Their distinctive dark spots are called rosettes, which help camouflage them when stalking prey. They are hunted for their fur.

AFRICAN LEOPARD

CRITICALLY ENDANGERED

The largest parrot in the world, with beautiful deep blue feathers and a yellow circle around each eye. It is poached for the illegal pet trade.

HYACINTH MACAW

The smallest species of bear in the world, they are jet-black with a patch of orange on their chest.

They are hunted for their meat, bones, teeth, claws, gall bladder and bile.

SUN BEAR

These turtles live in shallow lagoons and coral reefs where their armoured heads and shells protect them from jellyfish stings.

They are illegally traded for their eggs, meat, skin and shells.

HAWKSBILL TURTLE

TRAVEL ROUTE

JOURNEY TO AFRICA

START

4 HOUR JOURNEY

THE RED SEA

AGNES'S BEDROOM

THE NILE

DIAMOND McGLINTY GARAGE

DIAMOND McGLINTY'S GARAGE

PEREGRINE DRONE

SILVER BULLET BUGGY

CAIRO

CAIRO, EGYPT

FINISH

THE FLOWER'S SHREWS' BURROW

OPERATION: SANDWHISKERS

HOW CAN YOU HELP?

Raise awareness!

A great way to reduce the demand for illegal animal products is to better educate people about them. Why don't you ask your teacher if you can create a display at school to let people know more about the issue? You could use brightly coloured drawings, graphs and photos to make sure your display attracts attention. If you include a world map you could even draw lots of arrows on it, pointing to all the different countries where the threatened species live.

Check your holiday souvenirs!

When you or your parents go on holiday, check that the souvenirs you buy are not made from illegal animal products. Jewellery can be made from ivory, coral, tortoiseshell and rhino horn – all illegal materials. Some bags and shoes are made from reptile skin (yuck!) and fur shawls can be produced from endangered Tibetan antelope fur.

Sign petitions!

In the fight against the illegal animal trade, it's important to put pressure on governments to introduce tighter laws and better enforce their regulations. As well as signing petitions that call for change, you can write to your local MP and ask them what they plan to do about it.

Host an animal-tastic quiz!

Why don't you host an animal-themed quiz with your friends and family? You can charge a fee for every team taking part and bake an amazing cake as the star prize! You'll need to write the questions and keep the answers <u>well hidden</u>. Any money you raise can be donated to organizations who are actively working to dismantle the illegal animal trade, like The African Wildlife Foundation, WWF and TRAFFIC, the wildlife monitoring network. They support teams of anti-poaching rangers and place specially trained sniffer dogs along routes where wildlife products are being traded.

Good luck, agents!
SPEARS is relying on you.

Sincerely,

Commander Phil

JENNIFER BELL

Londoner Jennifer Bell worked as a children's bookseller and piranha-keeper at a world-famous bookshop before becoming an author. Her debut novel, *The Uncommoners: The Crooked Sixpence* was an international bestseller. **Agents of the Wild** is her first series for younger readers. She was recruited into **SPEARS** by a giant hairy armadillo named Maurice.

ALICE LICKENS

Co-creator Alice Lickens is an illustrator and author and a winner of the prestigious Sendak Fellowship for illustration. Her picture books include *Can You Dance to the Boogaloo?*, *How To Be A Cowboy*, and the Explorer activity book series with the National Trust. She joined **SPEARS** after receiving a tap on the shoulder from a Norwegian rat named Lorita.

Join **AGENTS OF THE WILD** on their other missions:

Species in danger? Girl and shrew to the rescue!